John Singer Sargent and Madame X

by Rosary Hartel O'Neill

A SAMUEL FRENCH ACTING EDITION

SAMUEL
FRENCH
FOUNDED 1830

NEW YORK HOLLYWOOD LONDON TORONTO

SAMUELFRENCH.COM

ISBN 978-0-573-69763-0   Printed in U.S.A.   #12584

MUSIC USE NOTE

IMPORTANT BILLING AND CREDIT REQUIREMENTS

CHARACTERS

JOHN SINGER SARGENT – 28, Handsome, a good athlete, formally dressed American. A bit naïve, he is courageous and daring and will defy everyone to protect his painting. No experience in love.

JUDITH GAUTIER – Late 20s, French art critic, beautiful. She champions artists and underdogs and admires Sargent.

CLAUDE MONET – 42, established landscape artist. A powerful art critic and teacher, he is working to improve his sensitivity to his students' struggles.

AMÉLIE GAUTREAU – 24, "Madame X." Exquisite. The most beautiful woman in Paris, she is from New Orleans and is having an affair with Dr. Possi.

DR. SAMUEL POSSI – (nicknamed Dr. Love - because of his promiscuity and the fame of his love room) Early 30s. He collects artists and destroys their souls and is enamored of Amélie Gautreau.

SARAH BERNHARDT – Mid 30s, the most famous actress in France, with a mother complex and a sexual history with Dr. Love.

EMILY SARGENT – 24, a delicate girl, with a childhood deformity. She is John Sargent's sister who follows him about and lives off his fame.

HENRY JAMES – Middle-aged, austere American novelist and critic living in England. He champions Sargent for his talent and is one of his greatest admirers.

OSCAR WILDE – 29, dapper Irish poet, living in London, dressed in dashing urbane attire. He believes in Sargent and the beautiful people of Paris and is always ready with a clever remark.

Possible doubles:

CLAUDE MONET and **HENRY JAMES**
OSCAR WILDE and **DR. LOVE**
JUDITH GAUTHIER and **SARAH BERNHARDT**
VICTOR HUGO and **RICHARD WAGNER** are walk-on with no lines.

SETTING

Multiple interior and exterior sets. Belle Époque Paris and London, 1882.

PROLOGUE THE LADY IN BLACK

(**AMÉLIE GAUTREAU** *appears in portrait pose & dress of Madame X)*

AMELIE. Welcome. I'm an exhibit. I'm the only living descendent of Madame X. I'm here to tell you beauty is more powerful than money, because I have it and I have had both. I had beauty long before I had money. My husband's money can't get me in anywhere I can't get myself in with beauty. I'm saying educated beauty, not like a sexy beauty. I fought real hard to maintain my position, to have beauty and class, as you will see.

(Lights fade. Lights go up on Stage Scene and Act One)

ACT ONE

Scene One

(DR. LOVE's salon, 10 Vendome Place, Paris. A rainy May afternoon. Offstage, **VICTOR HUGO** *reads from his novel and* **RICHARD WAGNER** *plays the piano. On stage in a silk kimono,* **JUDITH GAUTIER** *arranges Japanese flowers. She is beautiful, 37, full figure, large, expressive eyes.* **JOHN SARGENT** *rushes in under a dripping umbrella. Twenty-eight, he is handsome, robust, a good athlete, formally dressed.)*

JOHN. Amazing house.

JUDITH. It is the Doctor's "Palace of Creativity." Any artist who is anybody eventually comes here. *(Shakes his hand.)* Judith Gauthier.

JOHN. Daughter of the—

JOHN and **JUDITH.** Famed novelist.

JUDITH. And nun of art. *(Laughs, holding his hand.)* None in the morning, none in the evening.

JOHN. John Sargent. Student painter.

JUDITH. Rapidly ascending.

JOHN. I am here for a nomination—to the Salon.

JUDITH. Good luck.

JOHN. You are the critic who wrote that attack on me and—

JUDITH. Madame Gautreau from New Orleans. Yes, I am she.

JOHN. "Ambitious Americans seize our medals and glory."

*(***JOHN** *checks his pocket watch, peers out the rainy window. Two old men walk across the stage. One studies sheet music, the other a book.)*

JOHN. That's not... Victor Hugo and Richard Wagner.

JUDITH. I furthered their careers.

6

(Sound: Doorbell rings)

(CLAUDE MONET hurries in, drenched. Portly, he hides an artist's portfolio by the door.)

CLAUDE . Wicked out, rainy and cold.

JUDITH. Claude Monet. Let me introduce—

JOHN. We know each other.

JUDITH. *(To* **CLAUDE** *)* Your coat.

CLAUDE . *(Hesitates, coughs. Gives* **JUDITH** *his wet coat.)* It is too hot with it on, and too cold with it off. *(Pause)* Don't you go to class?

JOHN. I try to go. I went to the door. Did you bring the letter?

(CLAUDE coughs. Pounds his chest. Music from "The Ring Cycle" echoes offstage.)

JUDITH. Wagner. Playing catastrophically—

JOHN. (To **CLAUDE**) You come in panting.

(HUGO crosses, reading.)

CLAUDE . Victor Hugo! You know John Sargent?

(HUGO shakes **CLAUDE** *'S hand... profusely, never looking at* **JOHN***, exits.)*

JUDITH. Brandy?

CLAUDE . God, yes.

JOHN. Coffee. I don't want to be loose. I want to be tense.

(CLAUDE coughs and pounds his chest.)

CLAUDE. The Professor's dog died. He is not coming.

JOHN. Does he do this a lot?

7

CLAUDE . Some Frenchmen have never been nominated for the Salon.

JUDITH. John is from Philadelphia--

*(*JUDITH *exits.)*

CLAUDE . The Professor says, "Haven't we done enough for John already!"

JOHN. I didn't know I was out of favor?

CLAUDE . No one is in favor now.

JOHN. Artists, we are no better than squirrels. Spend all day looking for food.

CLAUDE . Hold off a year.

JOHN. Unlike you, I have no government stipend.

CLAUDE . The professor suggests you do Louise's portrait. She's social.

JUDITH. *(Pokes her head in.)* The school will get a commission.

CLAUDE . Here's that letter.

JOHN. It is in the handwriting of you-know-who. I don't want to touch it.

JUDITH. John shouldn't have to consider financing the Professor.

CLAUDE . *(Reads a paper)* He says: "If nominated, Sargent will have to organize the showing, pay all assistants and costs. If Louise's portrait sells, the studio will retain eighty percent."

JOHN. This is blackmail!

CLAUDE . Leverage. The Professor has got to—

JUDITH. Put his empire in place.

JOHN. The man wears the persona of genius without having done any of the work--

CLAUDE . My coat.

8

JOHN. Two hours of painting, thirty hours of eating and talking.

CLAUDE . *(Gives* **JOHN** *back his portfolio.)* Your submissions.

JOHN. Most students collect around him wanting a trade.

CLAUDE . In our world, rejection is the norm.

JOHN. I painted his first official portrait...

*(***JUDITH** *gives* **CLAUDE** *his coat. He turns to* **JOHN***.)*

CLAUDE . You don't realize how important the Salon is to the future careers of the stars of France. You are a newcomer. A neophyte. This competition was made to assist emerging French painters from the *Ecole des Beaux Arts.* The fact you, an American, are considered at all is unusual. Be satisfied. Many Parisians went out of their way to admit you into France's leading art school. We teach you and close our eyes. But now you want all the prizes. You aren't wise. Shouldn't it be enough that we include you with the French? You're not even European. Your family has no connections. They totter back and forth between countries, only arriving when the wealthy have left. Many artists are calling in favors to keep you at this state school. Now you want to be nominated to the premier competition with the top French youth. If you win, which you invariably might, how do we explain the school's use of state monies for your education? Why don't you exhibit in New York? Or come to Giverny. Do landscapes.

JOHN. Portraits are what I do.

*(***CLAUDE** *exits.)*

JUDITH. Why insist on entering the Salon?

JOHN. Employment depends on repeated proof of ability. Good art sells, but marketed well it sells better. The public must be reminded one striking performance isn't luck.

JUDITH. Your Professor is a dud, but don't let that fool you. He is a power in Paris.

JOHN. What should I do?

JUDITH. Paint a star.

(Sounds of crashing, crowds scream, soft crying.)

JOHN. Amélie Gautreau!

JUDITH. Getting out of her carriage before the doctor's office.

JOHN. What a luscious beauty. She looks fourteen.

JUDITH. She enters the best rooms in Paris.

JOHN. She's this weird binary opposition between promiscuity and classiness.

JUDITH. King Ludwig attended the Opera to see her climb the stair. Elizabeth of Austria posed her as a garden statue--

JOHN. How does such an American get touted the beauty of Paris. Don't tell me! She's a Civil War orphan from New Orleans—and the French have adopted her— I know I'm mesmerized too. Loveliness launched her into the world of power. Perhaps she could protect me. An American painting an American that the French might accept. Her beauty would entice Parisians to the portrait. So instead of being lost on the ceiling, it might be hung eye to eye. Amelie Gautreau there's a face could start a following.

Scene Two

(An anteroom in **DR. LOVE'S** *house.* **AMÉLIE GAUTREAU**, *24, enters. Exquisite, she suggests a Greek goddess, with an ample upturned bosom, narrow waist, long elegant neck, sculpted shoulders.* **DR. SAMUEL LOVE** *greets her. He is well-built, early thirties, with dashing good looks, and wears a close-fitting business suit.)*

AMÉLIE. Doctor!

DR. LOVE. It couldn't wait.

AMÉLIE. I forget I'm not your only flirtation.

DR. LOVE. You're the one that matters...Amélie!

AMÉLIE. I'm two months pregnant.

DR. LOVE. Holy Mother! Thank God you have a husband.

AMÉLIE. But, I've *marriage blanc* -- a sexless marriage. He's too old to--

DR. LOVE. Slip once, then have the baby. "Come early."

AMÉLIE. After my husband touches me, I vomit for twenty-four hours.

DR. LOVE. I'll give you a pill.

AMÉLIE. Couldn't you and I marry?

DR. LOVE. I'm married. You're married.

AMÉLIE. It's your baby. What should we do?

DR. LOVE. Say you're carrying your own vestigial twin. And --

AMELIE. Have an abortion? You said I wouldn't conceive--

DR. LOVE. I said bi-manual manipulation -- made termination painless. You've had good relations the first time.

AMELIE. But I want the baby.

DR. LOVE. The most beautiful woman in Paris can't be pregnant.

AMELIE. Talking to you is like speaking to a wall. I walk up and bang, hit my head.

DR. LOVE. Come here.

AMÉLIE. Don't touch me!

DR. LOVE. We can still have intercourse.

AMÉLIE. Good Lord! You are not even worried.

DR. LOVE. You won't show for months.

AMÉLIE. No, I would not expect you to feel for someone

DR. LOVE. My mother died at thirty-six, always pregnant.

AMÉLIE. Why should that concern me?

DR. LOVE. We don't want a scandal. Some innocent must be blamed. Perhaps a student...?

AMÉLIE. You must be insane.

DR. LOVE. I have nightmares about your confinement. I'm the son of a Protestant minister. I know the power of scandal. Some innocent must be blamed. A student like...

AMÉLIE. I won't do this.

DR. LOVE. We'll say while painting he fell for his model—

AMÉLIE. What about compassionate solutions–

DR. LOVE. Beautiful women are aphrodisiacs.

AMÉLIE. Surely there is another—

DR. LOVE. How about John Sargent, who's sitting next door?

AMÉLIE. I won't do th–

DR. LOVE. He's sexually naïve, American.

AMÉLIE. Don't even think--

DR. LOVE. He needs a star for his portrait and you're a candidate.

AMÉLIE. It's too convoluted.

DR. LOVE. Nothing's too deep for snakes not to move gracefully.

(Lights fade.)

Scene Three

(**DR. LOVE'S** *salon moments later.)*

(Lights up on **DR. LOVE** *entering.)*

DR. LOVE. Sam Pozzi. They call me Doctor Love. *(A corporeal glance passes between them)*

JOHN. John Sargent.

*(***DR. LOVE** *holds his hand a bit too long.* **JOHN** *withdraws it awkwardly)*
John Singer Sargent.

DR. LOVE. You are all dressed up–formal collar and cuff. You couldn't paint like that—

JOHN. It's important to give my canvas the respect it deserves.

DR. LOVE. You're civilized to the fingertips.

JOHN. Thanks, but I must go—

DR. LOVE. You don't socialize?

JOHN. I guard against time stealers.

DR. LOVE. Won't you look at my art? Indulge me. I am a hoarder. I'll add on a wing to the house *(Looks down.)* Here is a tortoise inlaid with gold and pearls. Marble from India, floors from Honduras, garnet-crusted frames. There is Degas, Monet, and your portrait of the Professor from last year's Salon.

JOHN. My! I never knew.

DR. LOVE. You are a national treasure waiting to be recognized.

JOHN. Don't exaggerate.

DR. LOVE. Or so Amélie thinks. I quote, "What to John is ordinary is to most painters—"

*(***AMÉLIE** *enters)*

AMÉLIE. Extraordinary.

JOHN. *(Awestruck)* Madame Gautreau!

AMÉLIE. John Sargent. I've heard of you by rumor. You have that man thing about you. Women want to say hello.

JOHN. *(Paralyzed seeing* **AMÉLIE***)* Amélie Gautreau.

AMÉLIE. Married to Pedro -- whatever his name is. I'm the other half. *(She puts out her hand. He pecks her.)* You've kissed your dog softer than you've kissed me.

DR. LOVE. Amélie may need a portrait.
(Exits.)

AMÉLIE. My husband is a millionaire in bat guano from Chile.

JOHN. So something ostentatious and grand? And the purpose of the portrait?

AMÉLIE. To replace children. Every chance he gets, Pedro jabs me about not wanting them.

JOHN. You could care less about that?

AMÉLIE. When I die, I die. In his case we live again through portraits.

JOHN. You don't believe that.

AMÉLIE. What does a good portrait involve?

JOHN. About two hundred hours of sitting.

AMÉLIE. I'd have to give up sixty parties. It's too time-consuming.

JOHN. You're forced to live that way to survive.

AMÉLIE. *(Cries)* I'm trying to do the sensitive thing that makes Pedro feel good--

JOHN. So you want full-length?

AMÉLIE. Can you paint my pure white skin? More marble than human.

JOHN. The musculature has vibrancy.

15

AMÉLIE. Capture how rice powder "spiritualizes" my flesh and carmine reddens my lips.

JOHN. Like in the paintings of Franz Hals.

AMÉLIE. Glorify my flawless skin?

JOHN. The Dutch artist.

AMÉLIE. It's all about spoiling myself for now. To combat wrinkles I stay a day a week in bed and apply creams all over my body. I bathe, bathe, and bathe again. I use pearl powder, violet powder, rouge, bisque for the eyelids, belladonna for the eyes, yellow shine and mineral potions for the hair. I varnish my face, fix on Russian ringlets, wear pre-Raphaelite dress. To make sure my gown won't clash with an interior, I make a trial visit to any house I'm invited to for a party...And your weakness as a painter?

JOHN. No personal life. Most parties bore me in ten minutes.

AMÉLIE. You protect your energy.

JOHN. Painting won't let me rest. My hands are always itchy.

AMÉLIE. I could feed your passion.

JOHN. How?

AMÉLIE. My greatest preoccupation is romance. Thank goodness for loose gowns in which a married woman can relax at five o'clock. Daytime fabric is heavy, like removing upholstery. The tea gown is as undressed as one can be in public and still be clothed. *(As if preparing to undo it.)* Below my robe I am seductively naked.

JOHN. I'm going to practice saying no. "No, no, no."

AMÉLIE. The most wonderful things are waiting on the other side.

Scene Four

*(The Salon continued. Crash offstage. **DR. LOVE** rushes in.)*

JOHN. An accident?

DR. LOVE. They wait to crash till they're near a doctor.

*(***HUGO** and* **WAGNER** *enter carrying John's sister,* **EMILY SARGENT**, *a pretty girl of 26, with a hunchback.)*

JOHN. My sister.

EMILY. *(Reaching for* **JOHN***)* You forgot your sketchbook.

JUDITH. She ran before the carriage.

EMILY. John! You're supposed to check with me.

DR. LOVE. Is she bleeding?

EMILY. I can't keep up with him.

JOHN. Are you in pain?

JOHN. *(to* **DR. LOVE***)* Is she bleeding? *(to* **EMILY***)* Are you in pain?

EMILY. I fell.

DR. LOVE. What part hurts?

EMILY. My...arm.

JUDITH. Can you move it?

EMILY. I'm fine. Did John get the nomination?

JOHN. Will Sis be all right?

JUDITH. I suspect. Coffee? *(***JOHN** *shakes his head.)* How long has she been--

JOHN. Following me? A few years. It's very sad. Everywhere I go, she tags after me. I tell her to make friends, but she hasn't found "her tribe." She's fragile, and accident-prone. She was dropped as a child. I was born first. Later children died. At birth, she could fit in a shoebox. (*Paces.*) Sis said a novena for me to win that nomination. But the path of glory is strewn with corpses. Mom has used up our savings. Papa's health is weak. What future awaits Sis if I fail? Marry a poor man with one foot. Let her husband's mistress move in. Her only distinction is her hair, so long she can sit on it. Hasn't cut it since she was born. She calls it her "too long to let hang hair."

JUDITH. I've seen girls like your sister in the wards of Charity Hospital.

JOHN. What's keeping the doctor?

JUDITH. She needs a goal because she'll never have a normal life.

JOHN. (*Paces, looking toward* **DR. LOVE** *'s office.*) I'm her purpose.

JUDITH. Good. We can both watch you paint, while she recuperates in my room.

JOHN. We couldn't inconvenience.

JUDITH. There's a wing for visiting artists.

(*DR. LOVE enters with* **EMILY***, who is wearing a sling.*)

DR. LOVE. Your sister's got a sprained arm. I waived my expenses.

EMILY. He gave me a ring with a single human teardrop.

JUDITH. (*To* **EMILY***.*) I'll braid your hair, put you in a kimono—

DR. LOVE. I need to watch her.

JUDITH. You and your brother can live here!

JOHN. I don't think so.

JUDITH. Don't you know about the balance teeter-totter?

EMILY. Let's stay. Please.

JUDITH. Maybe you've had so much badness; it's time for good...

*(Exiting with **EMILY**.)*

Scene Five

(Next week, at **DR. LOVE**'s. **AMÉLIE** *touches* **JOHN** *as they are going through trunks of costumes. She holds up a gown.)*

AMÉLIE. I love clothes but I loathe portraits.

JOHN. I won't impose my views.

AMÉLIE. Women put up with idiosyncrasies in wealthy artists, 'cause they get a lot—

JOHN. I'll make you even more beautiful.

AMÉLIE. But to be painted ten hours a day by a student.

(She turns away.)

JOHN. I'll immortalize you as the prettiest woman alive. Talk to me.

AMÉLIE. I can't.

JOHN. I need to see what you see. Be in your mind—your body. *(Pause)* Feel what troubles you?

AMÉLIE. Dark thoughts come into my head all the time so the rain won't let up.

JOHN. Was there a time when you didn't have these holes?

AMÉLIE. New Orleans was the cure. No one gets to be a big fish in Paris. It's too unforgiving. When I came here, it was not a welcoming place. This city doesn't have the flamboyance, the Caribbean feel New Orleans has. After the war, I brought my body to Paris, but I left my soul in New Orleans. There was thinness in my world there that allowed me to see possibilities. So many happy hours, days, months with my family beside the Mississippi River. I always felt I could go back and be the little girl and be protected. I guess no place that took you away from there is going to look good. But I've got to try not to care so much.

JOHN. You've always been displaced but now you're feeling it.

AMÉLIE. I've tapped into a rich gold vein here.

JOHN. Whatever, if you'll let me do the portrait.

JOHN. But you've shot your heart out.

AMÉLIE. I have to close my eyes; it's unreal.

JOHN. Your world is strife with black sins.

AMÉLIE. *(Pours a drink)* Let's get drowsy on champagne. What if I dislike something, like my left eye?

JOHN. Everyone has a skeleton in the closet, some ...

AMÉLIE. What if I hate the portrait?

JOHN. What if you love it?

AMÉLIE. I've never seen someone anticipate winning so quickly.

JOHN. We live not seeing our faces, so the other becomes a mirror.

AMÉLIE. But I don't want a—

JOHN. I'll give you one hundred percent attention.

AMÉLIE. Most men try to fashion you into something that works for them.

JOHN. You can do things while I paint.

AMÉLIE. Good. I'll daydream intensely, allow my body to open up, my imagination to soar. Fantasy makes you feel so nice. The visual interconnect with the skin, the sensory organs. Time stops. I like to dream. Doesn't matter if it's good or bad. I like to not think. *(Drinks.)* Counting time by heartbeats. You have to slow things down, focus on the body. Most people can't do that in their waking hours. They have to go to sleep—Me, I can do that standing in place. *(Drinks.)* Dreams are wishes. What would you do with a wishing well? You're so strong and sweet. Have you never loved a woman?

JOHN. I have a close family.

AMÉLIE. You choose to be isolated.

JOHN. I view others as interference.

AMÉLIE. It's easy to be alone, painting. But the inner voice never dies. You should stray. All affairs end. Some end in a day, a year. The next day, sometimes I feel real bad. I feel dirty because there has to be some bond. That's not true for most men...There's no permanent thing. There's different degrees of temporary.

JOHN. Let me paint you.

AMÉLIE. Fine. But this weight of platonic love has to be surgically removed from your brush.

(She caresses his cheek.)

Scene Six

(Later. **JUDITH**, **EMILY** *in a kimono enter with* **SARAH BERNHARDT**, *mid thirties, with wild golden hair.)*

JUDITH. The great Sarah Bernhardt.

EMILY. My. I used to follow you. Today it's called stalking.

SARAH. Gushing is always distasteful.

JOHN. Hello, Miss Bernhardt.

SARAH. I'm Sarah to the world, why shouldn't I be to you?

JOHN. Sarah.

SARAH. Singer Sargent. That's not French. I'm not going to beat about the bush.

AMÉLIE. 'Cause you don't have much bush to beat. Ha.

SARAH. Please! I'm Amélie's godmother and counselor. There are those who are family by birth and those who are family by acclamation. I've devoted myself to this girl's image. She wants to assimilate herself as quickly as possible to the appearance of a woman of a certain class. It's not easy. Soon as she got breasts men descended like bees to butter.

AMÉLIE. John is doing my portrait.

SARAH. You're going to put your face in the hands of an amateur? What do you say for yourself, Mr. John Singer? (*To* **JOHN**) I hear your father is a failed physician. Your mother a dilettante. Your sister a cripple.

JOHN. God! I need a pet that bites to show you how mean you are.

(Exits with **EMILY** *and* **JUDITH**.*)*
(Alone, **SARAH** *confronts* **AMÉLIE**.*)*

SARAH. You're headed for the guillotine. It's just a matter of when the cart gets there.

AMÉLIE. The doctor said John's portraits are good and original.

SARAH. Yes, but what's good is not original and what's original is not good.

AMÉLIE. I like him.

SARAH. You've bonded as expatriates do. Watch out. We don't need him all over you like applesauce. I don't trust men who are anarchists.

AMÉLIE. It's healthy to fight people who are not important.

SARAH. He was rejected from the Salon. Expunged!

AMÉLIE. You can't treat a—

SARAH. A portrait artist should be regenerative, enhance the face.

AMÉLIE. With John that's—

SARAH. Impossible. It is his own insistence on himself. He was home schooled and brought up with some woundedness around money. The only thing he'll reach for is your wallet. You can't be eccentric without being rich. Now, I've been painted thrice and each artist was wealthier than the last.

AMÉLIE. John's not dangerous.

SARAH. When you bring his name up, it polarizes the room. *(Pause)* When he's tested, he'll turn up violent; it's part of his life. He's always going to break out of the corral and head for the woods. He's like a wild horse. You can ride him for a while but then he'll have to buck you. Strengthen your bone character. Fire him. Let him beat the male drums. There is certain stability even in cruelty.

AMÉLIE. I'm so glad he's available

SARAH. You cannot stop birds of prey from flying overhead but you can stop them from nesting in your hair.

(She exits.)

(JUDITH and EMILY enter with HENRY JAMES and OSCAR WILDE dressed in dashing urbane attire.)

JUDITH. I would like to present our writers from Britain-Henry James and Oscar Wilde, who come with —

24

OSCAR. With letters, and occasional bunches of outrageous flowers.

HENRY. I didn't know a painter...could make me levitate.

(A bodily look goes from the men to **JOHN***, who turns away clumsily.)*

JOHN. I need to work.

OSCAR. I didn't know you had to struggle. I thought you just appeared.

HENRY. Your portraits are delicious!

OSCAR. I could eat them. And you're gorgeous! If you go into a city and they don't adore that outfit, get the hell out. During my last term at Oxford, I declared, "Reformation of dress is of far greater importance than reformation of religion." Tight lacing is bad both from the health and aesthetic points of view. A small waist gives no air of grace but exaggerates the width of the shoulders and hips. My motto is it's stupid to suffer for beauty. Why not suspend dresses from the shoulders and obviate the need for a corset? We all have these tummies. I look in the mirror and made my peace with it. Now I don't see it anymore.

JOHN. Why are you here?

OSCAR. We like beautiful things, being beautiful things ourselves.

JOHN. Seriously.

OSCAR. I don't like these gawking groups that watch plays and hang out at dinner.

HENRY. But anyone who is anybody passes through Dr. Love's Palace of Creativity.

OSCAR. I'm sure your cardiologist would never approve of what we do. *(Rolls his eyes.)* We gain some on the merry-go-round and lose some on the swings.

JOHN. I need to get back to work.

OSCAR. *(To* **HENRY***.)* I like him so much—

JOHN. Are you finished? To me, when a person takes my time, they steal my soul. Since I'm not famous, you don't value that. It's only by the sheer excellence of what I do, I can say I'm a painter. I'm damned pleased when my work gets hung. But then I've got to worry if anyone will buy it and like it. So to expand my appeal, I saturate myself with interesting people and double the amount of sittings.

OSCAR. Is he or isn't he?

HENRY. (To **OSCAR.**) I don't know why anyone would want to be androgynous.

OSCAR. Declare one side or the other. And—Hire a bodyguard at once.

HENRY. Paris is not a welcoming place. If you're from Philadelphia.

OSCAR. You get slapped with one hand and crowned with the other.

HENRY. Come to London.

JOHN. I know no one there.

OSCAR. Strangers are friends you haven't met.

HENRY. Rich Brits love money but they do squander it from time to time

EMILY. Wait! Could I have your autographs?

OSCAR. No. You've already got too much paper in your house. I'm afraid you'll die tragically. And John, if you end up having a tawdry affair with Amélie, would you call me at once. (*Kisses* **AMÉLIE's** *hand.*) You can always tell a bracelet by its garnets and a house by its finials. (*Shakes* **JOHN**'s *hand.*) I'll never touch your finial because it's next to your switch.

(**HENRY** *and* **OSCAR** *exit.* **EMILY** *and* **JUDITH** *follow them out.*)

Scene Seven

(Later. **JOHN** *and* **AMÉLIE** *look through a clothes trunk.)*

JOHN. Where shall we begin?

AMÉLIE. With the buttons. As a child, I wore gold buttons. See, here's my little white dresses from our plantation.

JOHN. Some things shouldn't be saved. You have to say it's finished.

AMÉLIE. Right. If you're living far from New Orleans, you can't miss it. When I broke through some of the really hard memories, I sobbed for days. All these thoughts hurried inside me. *(Takes liquor.)*

JOHN. Why are you drinking?

AMÉLIE. Because there's nothing wrong with it.

JOHN. You've got to snip negative thoughts.

AMÉLIE. I can't enjoy where I'm living because I'm too busy taking care of where I was.

JOHN. You have to develop something in you which allows you to grieve—

AMÉLIE. I can always go back to New Orleans.

JOHN. But not now.

AMÉLIE. After the acclaim of the portrait I'll do that.

JOHN. When you return "the most beautiful woman in Paris," you'll take New Orleans back.

AMÉLIE. Now it's filled with ghosts that could penetrate me.

JOHN. Right now they could. Mmmmm...I don't like the dress.

AMÉLIE. When I think about never going back to New Orleans, I could bawl. It was one of those places where if you had been transported by fairies and you woke up, within ten minutes, without asking a soul, you'd know where you were.

Sometimes out of the blue, I'm overcome with homesickness. I don't know where it comes from—Doc says maybe I act sad to control others.

JOHN. You like to see yourself surrounded by love.

AMÉLIE. Maybe. You prefer the blue shawl?

JOHN. You should feel good about yourself without anyone else.

AMÉLIE. That's a weakness to need people...

JOHN. Try the pink cape. I'd think you'd take joy from your looks.

(She changes before him.)

AMÉLIE. Beauty rarely gives me enough. Men take me from the box, unwrap the tissue, let me out, wrap me up, put me back in the box.

JOHN. Try another dress.

(She does.)

AMÉLIE. How will you choose?

JOHN. The composition must be right for your soul. *(Pause)* I'm happier when I come here than I was at the studio where I studied. Whenever I went there, someone threw a lance at my stomach. Then I sensed arrows coming before I walked in. I can't return there honorably because it's steered by cowards. I survived, because I don't need praise. We're too American to be totally admired.

AMÉLIE The portrait will change that.

JOHN. Most people have chiseled success from a bedrock of pain.

AMÉLIE. If you were to claim your laurels—

JOHN. I'd go find passionate work elsewhere.

AMÉLIE. But they're hanging you at the Salon.

JOHN. Your beauty, not my name.

AMÉLIE. For now. When you started sketching me, the voice said—"Things will change." I've progressed more in four days than I have in twenty years. I can make my own decisions. I'm not always asking others to tell the good little girl what to do.

JOHN. You did that?

AMÉLIE. Relationships were too confusing

JOHN. Men love you because you shine gentleness and they want to experience that.

AMÉLIE. I like it when we're alone.

JOHN. Do you?

AMÉLIE. This is my prayer, so you can take as long as you want to answer. Come to my chateau in Brittany. It's the first place I went to by myself. There's a spacious walled park filled with oak trees. In the country, the mind has more juice. You can listen to the crickets, watch the flowers grow, and allow yourself the pleasure of overwork.

JOHN. Fine. I did so much not painting this week I'm exhausted.

(They kiss.)

Scene Eight

(Two months later: **AMÉLIE***'s chateau, Les Chenes Parame, Brittany. He wraps her naked in a sheet to paint her.* **DOCTOR LOVE** *arrives.)*

DR. LOVE. Where is—your husband?

AMÉLIE. Mexico. We like seeing him once a month.

DR. LOVE. Enjoy your independence.

AMÉLIE. I'll be in a cage soon enough.

DR. LOVE. *(Trying to kiss her.)* Don't I rate a kiss?

AMÉLIE. John dislikes when I leave my pose.

DR. LOVE. How precious; the model is so devoted.

JOHN. You're being funny?

DR. LOVE. No, I'm being mean.

DR. LOVE. Excuse us—

JOHN. *(Bitterly.)* I'd prefer not to.

*(***JOHN** *leaves. She collapses on a bed.)*

AMÉLIE. Well, what do you think?

DR. LOVE. I have multiple personalities, and none of them like him.

AMÉLIE. You are jealous.

DR. LOVE. John is macho and prissy, traits that make a man obnoxious.

AMÉLIE. He's acrid, true—

DR. LOVE. Bourgeois at best. The middle class is on top of all this molten lava of hatred.

AMÉLIE. I let him go by me like bad weather. As soon as we met, it was not a question of if, it was a question of where... These Capricorn men can be so difficult. And there is definitely a lot of lesson stuff in Capricorn Alpha males for me! All three of the really important men in my life...Capricorn! And I'm an Aquarius Rising, which is almost the same as being a Capricorn myself. Inevitable minor clashes. So...we'll see if John is mellow enough, or if he chooses to pout...I hope not. I go crazy without him...and truth to tell, he without me, 'cause when he is pouting I get all his erotic energy in the brief before bed/getting up personal time he allows himself—yes, it comes down to how he deals with painting...and that's fine...then his family...and that's a habit, and... By the end of the day, his 6:30 a.m. to 11:30 p.m. days!...he can hardly relax...so it takes a bit of doing to chisel that open. I'm utterly clear he loves me...and trusts me...but his pace when painting is different than mine, and it frustrates him.

DR. LOVE. You can't quit your obligations.

AMÉLIE. I tried to tell him but—You have no idea the sacrifices he makes—

DR. LOVE. I've tickets to the ballet...

AMÉLIE. Isolation is required.

DR. LOVE. People will forget you!

AMÉLIE. When John paints best, he feels purged—

DR. LOVE. Painters act superior because they spend the day in contemplation.

AMÉLIE. They are superior.

DR. LOVE. This man's a parasite.

AMÉLIE. A recluse, painting me eighteen hours a day.

DR. LOVE. I've bought portraits from his type and once they had me, they bloody screwed me.

AMÉLIE. You don't enjoy much of what artists offer, because—I'm not criticizing—you dislike contemplation.

DR. LOVE. I've the biggest art collection in Paris.

AMÉLIE. With John, I feel totally alive. It's exciting to be in a place where things are birthing.

DR. LOVE. Have you told him about the pregnancy?

AMÉLIE. *(Dreamily)* This portrait is my way to become the person I am meant to be.

DR. LOVE. If something happens with this—

AMÉLIE. *(Drinks from a small vial.)* John's like the astrologer exploring my world with a telescope. He wishes to know who I am fully. He sees deep inside my beauty and says I'm an enchantress. *(Drinks more.)* Somehow through the portrait we both live more profoundly.

DR. LOVE. *(Takes the vial.)* How much arsenic have you been taking?

AMÉLIE. Enough to turn lavender without killing myself.

DR. LOVE. Ye Gods!

AMÉLIE. Peacocks eat poison to make their tails bright.

DR. LOVE. You need to be conservative within the confines of your eccentricities.

DR. LOVE. When will you tell John about the baby?

AMÉLIE. He knows. John is very attached and that's not a bad thing.

DR. LOVE. *(Puts a hand on her stomach.)* You are starting to deform.

AMÉLIE. Tighten my corset.

DR. LOVE. The most beautiful woman can't be fat.

AMÉLIE. Ooh, I'll squeeze in. I won't add an inch.

DR. LOVE. That's my girl. Does this hurt?

AMÉLIE. No, pull more. *(She grits her teeth in pain.)* I don't know how to function as a mother. I've gotten rid of so many people I feel like a dead person. A child can be quiet and dumb and still get her way. But can a mother?

DR. LOVE. Kiss me.

AMÉLIE. Not now.

DR. LOVE. Oh no, am I the ex-boyfriend?

AMÉLIE. I have no strength.

DR. LOVE. Who knows if the painting will even be worth hanging?

AMÉLIE. I'm going to purchase it for thousands of dollars.

DR. LOVE. No. You've fallen into the vortex of flattery. I'm lucky I've never been that tempted. Has John decided on the pose? No? That's dire. You have boxed yourself into such a black corner. All you can do is cut your way out the backside. You'll have to take whatever he gives you now.

AMÉLIE. I can't waste time with you.

DR. LOVE. You said beneath my coat I had wings—

AMÉLIE. If I need you for something I'll tell you. If I do not...tell you. I do not need you...for whatever you were...hoping I would...

DR. LOVE. How much have you been drinking?

AMÉLIE. I do not mind...getting drunk on good champagne but I do not want to- *(DR. LOVE yanks corset.)* My God. You're hurting me. Stop! *(AMÉLIE has violent cramps.)* Mercy. Oh no. Help.

(JOHN walks in, pulls DR. LOVE and AMÉLIE apart.)

JOHN. Are you hurt?

AMÉLIE. Oh! I'm –

DR. LOVE. Bleeding.

JOHN. Oh, No!

AMÉLIE. It's awful. The pain. Oh Lord!

JOHN. You're turning blue.

DR. LOVE. She is hemorrhaging, fool.

AMÉLIE. I am giving birth to a pure viper.

DR. LOVE. Quiet.

AMÉLIE. *(Screams at* **DR. LOVE.***)* Like you.

JOHN. What's wrong?

DR. LOVE. Help! Lift her to the bed.

JOHN. She's having a...

DR. LOVE. My baby!

CURTAIN

ACT TWO

Scene One

(The chateau, Brittany. Two days later. **JOHN** *paces. Wailing offstage.* **JUDITH** *and* **EMILY** *enter.)*

EMILY. I brought you paints.

JUDITH. The Doctor is giving Amélie a— He is cutting off his appendage, as he calls it. She acts sad but inside she is saying, "Yes."

EMILY. They pretended the baby was yours.

*(***EMILY** *runs out.)*

JOHN. *(Looks about)* Where is my suitcase? *(Looks around for it. Finds it and starts stuffing his things into it.)*

JUDITH. They are killing it, but it wasn't yours.

JOHN. I get a few arrows in me and I fly. Otherwise they'll keep shooting at me.

(Sound: More offstage wailing.)

JUDITH. You can't leave!

JUDITH. The Salon's coming up.

JOHN. I was naïve and I had my soul crushed and –

JUDITH. You didn't see Amélie the way she was but the way you were.

JOHN. I walked into wolves naked and let them chew –

JUDITH. The woman was duplicitous.

JOHN. *(He keeps packing.)* I never had a girl because deep inside I knew the pain involved. I had so much in my life, passion for my work, my friends, family.

JUDITH. If I thought I was losing you, I would fight for you. I would walk through fire for you.

JOHN. Amélie was ...

JUDITH. The reason we get distraught when our lover goes, we think God has left; but God hasn't left, a human being has. Paint.

JOHN. I can't bludgeon myself to do it.

JUDITH. Feeling will come out your brush and flood onto the canvas.

JOHN. I cannot find a satisfactory pose. I sketched her seated with her head raised, then lowered, playing the piano. I did a watercolor of her with a book and a brisk oil of her holding champagne. I drew her kneeling on a sofa looking out the window. Nothing worked. The only way to redeem her portrait is to burn it.

JUDITH. Even if Amélie loved you, she could die—

JOHN. When the doctor took her off, I knew it'd never be the same. Suddenly she's with this –

*(Sound: More screaming. **EMILY** runs in)*

EMILY. She has been trying to kill the baby.

JOHN. God.

EMILY. Three of Mother's babies died, but she wanted them to live.

(Sound: Wailing offstage)

JUDITH. Paint Amélie at my chateau next door.

JOHN. Other women I can draw as a clinician, but Amélie I could only do as a dreamer.

JUDITH. Don't quit.

JOHN. Her portrait is about something that didn't happen.

JUDITH. Well, draw something that did.

JOHN. Most of us can only let so much go at a time. It's a terrifying process to let the old life go and experience something you've no idea where it is going to take you.

JUDITH. Most women are existing, not living. Reflect how you feel now.

Scene Two

(The chateau, moments later. **JOHN** *walks to a window.* **AMÉLIE** *enters.)*

JOHN. Amélie!

AMÉLIE. How did you know?

JOHN. I was used by girls when I was younger and discarded.

*(***JUDITH** *and* **EMILY** *exit.)*

AMÉLIE. Forgive me, John. The sun is coming up over the horizon, a red orb.

JOHN. You get this love experience from nature.

AMÉLIE. From you.

JOHN. Interesting artists are distractions.

AMÉLIE. You glided into my life like some god man.

JOHN. They come, they go.

AMÉLIE. And when I thought you loved me—I merged with you and I was—happy.

JOHN. That wasn't the real you. That was a performance.

AMÉLIE. You loved it here. Being in the beauty.

JOHN. You are my world everywhere. When you suffer, I cannot sleep. I go to the shore and listen to the waves crashing, until the screeching sea-gulls wake me up. When you are blue, I ruminate...three hundred sixty thought-degree circles. I shouldn't paint this, do that. Now I want to be sad. I want to walk with a chip on my shoulder. Because no one cares about me.

AMÉLIE. You worry all the time?

JOHN. Now I use evidence. It's called implication, evidence and extrapolation.

AMÉLIE. Maybe I haven't gone completely—my body still works. Thank God.

JOHN. How could you kill the –

AMÉLIE. It was damaged. Not a person. My body rejected it.

JOHN. A baby can't defend itself because it's dead—

AMÉLIE. My chemistry wasn't there to handle it.

JOHN. It can't come back, say you did it wrong.

AMÉLIE. Doctor says our genes are programmed for grim consequences.

JOHN. Do I have a gene for insanity?

AMÉLIE. Don't feel bad. I wasn't a mother. I was someone who was transformed into—I'd long since departed to some far-away place. There was no growing in me, just beautiful emptiness...I'm not supposed to think of the baby, and you shouldn't either.

JOHN. Why is it the male should not be soft and the female can be ruthless, cold-hearted, downright mean?

AMÉLIE. Because the female controls that power.

JOHN. You are shrewd, although you like to present yourself as fluff and mirrors.

AMÉLIE. I can barely speak when I look at you. Even now, miserable and bleeding, all I want to do is hold you naked... *(She drinks.)* I love watching the champagne bubble. It is like spirits dancing across water, now it is sparkling.

JOHN. Is that why you indulge yourself in it so much? To wipe that sorry feeling out?

AMÉLIE. Once you have had morphine, alcohol is nothing. Just a garnish. *(Quietly to* **JOHN.**) Do you want some?

JOHN. I suppose the baby died a horrible, neglected death.

AMÉLIE. My body self-destructed. Our bodies tell us what to do, if our minds won't. *(Long pause. She drinks.)* Until today, the Doctor hadn't offered to sponsor my portrait. Every so often he sent out a feeler, tested the waters. Paris is not just a Mecca for beauties and painters, but also for arts patrons eager for fame.

It is hard for him to give you glory like that. Now he feels sorry for me, and he'll help. Not think of --Oh, John. Won't you finish the portrait —

JOHN. Lots of portraits were painted that shouldn't have been. Lots of canvas bleached in vain.

AMÉLIE.—now we know it will be well placed? Paint me—in this. I feel the need for the quiet of black.

JOHN. It's a treacherous gown.

AMÉLIE. Waiting for an enchantress. Half ghost, half cat! I used you. Forget about me think about the portrait. It could launch your career. I'll get it featured in the best room in that Salon. People will worship your talent. Oh let me. I know how to do this. When you hear the rush of that opening crowd you'll forgive me.

JOHN. I shall need to do something dreadful to that dress. Rip off a strap. Now twist in profile, hold that. I think I've got something. Now talk...about...romance

(He starts to draw her.)

AMÉLIE. For good intimate relations you have to have champagne or rudimentary love. A fleeting feeling—crystallized through the fire of experience. I like the release flashes that go off in my brain; I also like to hear a man scream. It makes me feel I've a purpose, to help him become free.

JOHN. I have never felt free.

AMÉLIE. You should let yourself go. Tie in with nature from millions of years ago. If you give up all the barriers and feel your primeval rushes, you are going to release good and hard.

JOHN. Stand by that table. I will draw you with my brush...beginning with the shadows...and gradually evolving...your profile from the background by means...of large, loose volumes of shade, half-tones...of light, refinements of form, finally...bringing the masses of light...and shade closer together, and assembling your true figure.

AMÉLIE. Say you love me, John, say it now. You love me! Love me.

Scene Three

(**AMÉLIE** *is alone, drugged, drinking.* **DR. LOVE** *enters*)

DR. LOVE. Get up! I want my morphine back...a week's supply is enough.

AMÉLIE. (*Hyper*) Don't disturb the quiet of the . . .

DR. LOVE. (*Checks bottle*) You took arsenic too...? How much...Answer!

AMÉLIE. It's amazing what tone I let you...use with me...when I... (*Drinks*) I've huge... I don't remember stuff. (*Drinks*) Tell me how the baby died. I need to be sad.... I wanted you to... tighten my belt, create a curved shape. (*Clock chimes.*) Tick tock... ti...I suppose it just wound down like--there was no sound left in the music box. My bab...the thing...was... (*Sobs*) It was too little; it had no ability to grow. Omygod! Omygod! (*Drinking, wine*) I love *Veuve Cliquot* more...than life. (*laughs*) Parenting is for the middle part of life, 30-40. ...

(**DR. LOVE** *opens a basket of food*)

DR. LOVE. We'll picnic inside. It's rained enough to make it hotter. I brought *pate de fois gras.*

AMÉLIE. Nice how you serve food—

DR. LOVE. It's still France. I come from people who sat at table for one meal and talked about the next. (*Pause, stern*) Pick up your fork.

AMÉLIE. Why start? I don't think I've ever left a meal where I felt full—

DR. LOVE. You can't keep drinking.

AMÉLIE. (*Toasts him*) Juicing up for my sitting.

DR. LOVE. Fine. I won't eat either. Take the nuts away. Take the wine away. (*Examining her*) You need air. Let's go for a walk. Your garden is--

AMÉLIE. --a Darwinian experiment. I'm waiting to see if it can survive without any attention. (*Clock chimes.*) Tick. Tock (*Sobs*)

DR. LOVE. How long has John been painting? 2 months? He's a 2 month old. How long has--?

AMÉLIE. 139 years. *(Pause)* He's almost finished.

DR. LOVE. Do you like the portrait?

AMÉLIE. *(Hyper)* John paints in... black silence.

DR. LOVE. You haven't seen it? You must. Let him paint what satisfies you, and I'll see he wins the competition. I have to go back to Paris, grease the power list. Now give me the morphine I loaned you. *(She does so reluctantly.)*

At the beginning leisure is your friend not your enemy.

(DR. LOVE exits. Sound of rain.)

(JOHN enters with coffee. AMÉLIE stumbles to her pose, singing)

AMÉLIE. *(Sings, flirtatiously)* "Once there were greensleeves, kissed by the sun. Once they were valleys—"

JOHN. Drink this coffee. Focus. Oh no. You spilled it. You've been in the bottle —

AMÉLIE. One time, only one time. *(Slips)* Come blot my dress. *(Points to her chest)* Oops. *(Stands up unsteadily)* CATCH ME. Whee. Is this day special enough for that *Veuve Cliquot?*

JOHN. Fix your arm. Your dress. Swan neck. Stand back by the table. Contort the wrist.

AMÉLIE. Can I talk about whatever I want?

JOHN. If you'll hold that pose.

AMÉLIE. Oh let me talk about the baby. I'll drink the coffee. *(Drinks)* I've great muscle memory. I'll follow the 50 percent rule. I'll talk 50 percent less. I didn't believe the baby was... real because it had never... lived before... My insides were full of fear and bleeding...I couldn't balance but I... *(Drinks)* It was the ...the *(Drinks)* summer of death. Ha... I read that somewhere... Shush! The baby was......it was from the devil. Talk to me. Don't go inside the painting.

JOHN. Shut up. That's an order. Twist your arm more.

AMÉLIE. Why?

JOHN. *(Crazed focused on his painting)* Startling contrast is what art is about.

AMÉLIE. Ouch! Before—we took a break—can't we drink out the same cup like--

JOHN. *(Screams)* No, Medusa! It's amazing I can still be in the same room with you.

AMÉLIE. I won't pose anymore if you don't fix my hair, my bodice...Lift my gown...

JOHN. No...

AMÉLIE. I think my chin is wrong-Turn it!

JOHN. No. *(Angry)* I lose focus when you're close. You're too tensed up ...impossible

AMÉLIE. I'm forgetting my pose...the way I should stand...spread my lips--.

JOHN. MOVE BACK. My body is mine and I'll – This is the one thing you can't have! You're a rich spoilt bitch that lives on the support of others. A parasite. I'm running around your castle painting with numb fingers trying to keep the holes in my heart from leaking on the canvas and you're sitting in your queen chair holding court. Only your portrait has *gravitas.* *(Pause)* After the portrait is complete and acclaimed-- Maybe then . . . I'll get--

AMÉLIE. Your love back? Make me beautiful! Then you'll forget all this! I'll be your . . . immortality. We'll do a series of portraits. No one loves painting Amélie Gautreaux more than John Singer Sargent.

Scene Four

(**DR. LOVE**'s *Salon;* **CLAUDE** *and* **DR. LOVE** *enter)*

DR. LOVE. How could he paint her like that? Unattainable beauty reduced to narcissism.

CLAUDE. Even so, I admire it.

DR. LOVE. Part of him hated her.

CLAUDE. The portrait is a retreat from previous submissions.

DR. LOVE. His colors are somber, his brushwork too finished, and his conception simplistic and unflattering.

CLAUDE. You're sleeping with her again. Ah! The highest trades are in bed.

DR. LOVE. After he came back to Paris, he went back into—

CLAUDE. Sargent is going to follow his instincts and damn the world.

DR. LOVE. I tried to reason with him over dinner. Impossible.

CLAUDE. He's refuses to rein in his style.

DR. LOVE. The man steals all his images.

CLAUDE. Yes, but he steals with genius. Sargent's rise has been a magnificent steady –

DR. LOVE. This is where your little locomotive runs off track—Manet's "Olympe" was knifed because he painted a real woman nude. Sargent is headed for disaster—if he doesn't tone down the painting.

CLAUDE. Should we warn him?

DR. LOVE. Go to maids' quarters in an eighth-floor walk-up?

CLAUDE. I'll go alone.

DR. LOVE. Actually, bad reviews could help you. Surely it troubles you his name is mentioned twice as much as yours. John could win your government stipend. Why not mentor him in landscapes?

CLAUDE. He doesn't want to change.

DR. LOVE. Aren't you on the steering committee?

CLAUDE. I can't let personal feelings interfere with—

DR. LOVE. I'm not asking you to vote against the portrait. I'm saying you could talk to a few people. Tell them about—well, colleagues find him vitriolic. Once, resenting a silence, he slashed a canvas with a sword and roared out of the studio.

CLAUDE. Still, he has the appeal of a romantic mystery. From his arrival, he provided a spectacle of energy unleashed.

DR. LOVE. Oh no, here he comes.

(JOHN *enters.*)

JOHN. Have you seen my portrait?

CLAUDE. I've studied it.

JOHN. Good. I don't feel a painting lives till my friends view it.

CLAUDE. It's clear you admire Tintoretto.

JOHN. I was dissatisfied and dashed some pink over the—

DR. LOVE. Gloomy background.

JOHN. Vast improvement, don't you agree?

CLAUDE. Yes—I mean, perhaps.

JOHN. I played down the urge to localize my sitter.

DR. LOVE. But why give the starring role to clothes?

JOHN. What do you mean?

45

DR. LOVE. And such colors?

CLAUDE. Raisin and claret-soaked plum.

DR. LOVE. Were you thinking of a fruit compote?

JOHN. Why the slap?

DR. LOVE. Let's hope the portrait expands your clientele beyond expatriate Americans.

JOHN. Amélie's gotten me the biggest room in the Salon. The painting will be hung at eye level. People will see how focused we Americans can be. If the portrait is successful critics won't control which paintings get seen and which get skied.

DR. LOVE. No one will like her like this.

JOHN. Fine. It's the way she was, wanting to be loved, trail-blazing toward it. The black goddess is what she's became.

Scene Five

(*The Awards Ceremony,* **DR. LOVE**'s *Salon, later.* **CLAUDE,** *backed by the doctor, stands at a podium.* **AMÉLIE, JOHN, SARAH, EMILY, JUDITH, OSCAR, HENRY** *and stand-ins* **WAGNER** *and* **HUGO** *fill the audience.* **JUDITH** *and* **EMILY** *run to the podium.*)

JUDITH. You people are a testament to the importance of John's talent.

JOHN. (*To* **EMILY.**) I've got the flies.

EMILY. We're moving into the A crowd.

AMÉLIE. I can't get enough exposure.

DR. LOVE. You lap it up like chocolate. (*Squeezes* **AMÉLIE's** *arm.*) Right?

CLAUDE. Come here, John. Tell us about your work. Ladies and gents. John Singer Sargent.

JOHN. I start every morning; painting hours at a time. My plan is to make a complete sketch, which dries so rapidly that the next morning I might paint another study over it. I want to paint what my eye sees, not what my mind instructs me to see.

CLAUDE. You may recall Sargent's portrait of Professor Duran provoked much interest. Today's work was judged by forty critics—including the amazingly decadent, desperate but still whimsical Oscar Wilde and Henry James.

OSCAR. We're here. We're wanting—

HENRY. And we're ready to be amazed.

CLAUDE. Our master of ceremonies is Dr. Sam Love. To continue, Sargent strides deep into that territory called influence. He has set out on the trail of light, of strong contrast. (*Pause*) Envelopes require someone to open them, and Miss Bernhardt's hands are it.

SARAH. Sarah!

(**CLAUDE** *passes her an envelope, which she reads.*)

SARAH. *(Cont.)* Oh my! "The painting looks monstrous and decomposed? Indecent!"

DR. LOVE. *(Taking over.)* "He has placed the subject in a sorry dark pool."

JOHN. It's just one notice—

DR. LOVE. "People find the portrait atrocious."

OSCAR. *(Calls out.)* For me it is a perfect painting.

DR. LOVE. "Sargent has made Mme. Gautreau horrible in daylight." *(Reads more.)* "He paints her ears rose, her hair mahogany; her eyebrows in dark thick lines, her white shoulders disgust us." *(Reads.)* "The fallen strap reeks of decadence."

(Sounds of heckling. **DR. LOVE** *defers notices to* **CLAUDE***)*

CLAUDE. *(Reads.)* "The profile is pointed, the eye microscopic!"

AMÉLIE. I'll die of shame.

CLAUDE. "The right arm lacks articulation, the hand is deboned."

AMÉLIE. Let's go, John—

JOHN. I want to hear it.

CLAUDE. *(Reads.)* "Detestable! Boring! Monstrous! 'Madame X' lacks technique." *(Sounds of people rushing.)* Order! *(Louder noises.)* Ladies and Gentlemen.

*(***JOHN** *goes to leave.* **AMÉLIE, SARAH**, *and the doctor stop him.)*

DR. LOVE. Are you sick?

JOHN. You don't have to be sick to die.

CLAUDE. You owe Amélie a public apology.

JOHN. *(Removes sword.)* Artists have to be vigilant and have weapons. You critics live in the dirt, the muck, and we have to let you know we're going to stand up to you and kill you. But artists shouldn't have to battle. We shouldn't have to be brutes to survive. Oh yeah, it's OK, mock my painting. I'm fine.

DR. LOVE. Take down your portrait.

JOHN. No.

DR. LOVE. You'll have to fight me.

JOHN. So!

JUDITH. *(To* **JOHN.***)* You'll hurt your hands!

JOHN. Fine. My portrait stays in Room 31, at the Salon Competition!

DR. LOVE. I say it comes down.

JOHN. You'd like to squash me along with the hundreds of artists you've erased— creeping up to their attics, embracing failure in a bottle. I want to tell the painters in Paris, the Americans, the Mongoloids, the Turks that for every three thousand artists you critics level they'll be one John Singer Sargent who raises his painting on the pedestal and says "It's not garbage, it's great."

*(***JOHN** *and* **DR. LOVE** *fight.* **DR. LOVE** *pulls out a knife.* **JOHN** *shoves him back, leaves.)*

JOHN. Move, or I'll bludgeon you to death!

(Light: Blackout.)

Scene Six

(JUDITH, EMILY, OSCAR, HENRY *at a graveyard in London.)*

HENRY. I know what the controversy was in Paris. It's all about the ripped strap on her dress, the violated attire. We have to do something.

OSCAR. Why is that so shocking?

HENRY. John broke a primal rule in portraits – never defile a client.

JUDITH. We can't let him give up hope and...

OSCAR. ...go sit in some godforsaken London graveyard.

JUDITH. I thought he was staying with you.

EMILY. He's humiliated, can't face anybody.

HENRY. It's discouraging to see promising artists do themselves in.

EMILY. I know. I know! Some see their faculties going and blow their heads off. Others tie stones to themselves and drown. Some drink themselves to death. Some famous ones whose lives are unspeakable choke to death on drugs, and sleep in their own feces.

HENRY. Surely there are critics like me who appreciate the painting.

OSCAR. The swanlike, pre-Raphaelite dress.

JUDITH. Bad reviews can't last more than three weeks in the public mind.

EMILY. The portrait is still up.

JUDITH. More critics can review it.

HENRY. The curiosity factor is on our side.

JUDITH. We must contact other critics.

HENRY. How about the London Gazette?

JUDITH. Good. They only allow professionals to critique.

OSCAR. Because they don't feel students should be led by the blind.

EMILY. I know an art reviewer in Normandy.

OSCAR. I've an old lover in Brittany.

JUDITH. I once reviewed in Dublin.

HENRY. And I in London.

OSCAR. I've a close cousin in Scotland.

HENRY. If we create enough controversy, everyone will want to judge for themselves.

EMILY. Certainly some people do not like the doctor.

OSCAR. I'll contact his enemies.

HENRY. We will change the opinion of "Madame X."

JUDITH. One critic at a time.

Scene Seven

(A graveyard, London. **JOHN** *sits on a tomb, sketching.* **DR. LOVE** *enters in a heavy coat.)*

DR. LOVE. Why are you hiding out in London? You'll catch your death.

JOHN. The only thing I can control is myself and I've a tenuous hold on that.

DR. LOVE. You're living on a grave?

JOHN. I sit on a different tomb to draw each day. Those tombs are unmarked and I want to enjoy each one.

DR. LOVE. You are a warrior. That's fascinating.

JOHN. I'm an alien. The Salon took away my claws. I've got to get my power back.

DR. LOVE. John, I hope you don't mind if I polish my walking stick while we have a final talk.

JOHN. I do.

DR. LOVE. *(Polishes stick.)* Your eccentricity is causing questions in the legal department of the Salon. People are not sure who you are. When I agreed to sponsor your portrait, I thought it was just for you to hang it and avail yourself of some services, but you've gone too far. Hold back—maybe participate in one of the lectures. People know your work, they've seen your painting, don't be so eager to push it at others. Several people have come to me and asked me who you are to be going to England like this. I certainly like your charm and enthusiasm for your work and I don't want you to lose that, but you should withdraw the portrait.

JOHN. You are a devious rat. Soon as you got with the Salon's Board of Directors, you voted down my painting. There are twice as many negative adjectives in the dictionary as positive ones. I cringe when I hear how you people talk. You are abusive; irrational –

DR. LOVE. If you are going to attack, give me a day so I can get a crowd.

JOHN. Critics. Rather than develop your abilities, you are going to find ways to abort artists. We don't always know when it'll happen. You take away the artists who are outside your vision and promote losers. It's pre-Civil War management. "Bury the slaves in insults until they scream."

DR. LOVE. Do you know whom you're fighting? Bernhardt, Wagner, Monet, Hugo—

JOHN. The weak never attack unless they have overwhelming numbers. It's a turf war. You all got together over coffee in an unspoken conspiracy against me. The way I dress, the way I act. You figured I was moving in. You smelled me a mile. You're a snake. Snakes merge with the leaves. Look like they are leaves until they move.

DR. LOVE. *(Calls out.)* Sarah! Talk some sense into this moron.

(SARAH enters. DR. LOVE exits. JOHN hides behind a tomb.)

SARAH. I don't know where you are. It's exciting that you're not to be found.

JOHN. The torture continues.

SARAH. Things here are quiet. People do not seem to be around you the way I expected.

JOHN. One tomb to the other. That's about it.

SARAH. The press flatly denounced Amélie's appearance! Nothing could be said worse than has been said in "Le Monde."

SARAH. So the best of the young professionals leaves France.

JOHN. They don't notice their shelves are bare because they have eaten everything and are fat.

SARAH. I don't like you, but you're the only one who can paint. You can't imprint these fools with standards if you don't come back. You were one of the lynch pins that kept the Salon exciting. So you're staying in England.

JOHN. Sometimes I go across into Ireland.

SARAH. Relocation takes a big emotional bite.

JOHN. I like it here—with my friends who don't know me. My parents never settled down. We had no idea whom we might see from year to year. So I am undaunted by a new country.

SARAH. But to be alone for days, it stratifies, ossifies, hardens you. I still remember your pride as you accompanied...

JOHN. Amélie through the little Salon gate.

SARAH. Return to Paris—withdraw the portrait. The portrait means more to her than you. There you put all your talent, but she put all her fame. *(Pause)* The portrait had a line before it all week. I dodged behind doors to avoid friends who looked grave. I took Amélie to see it by the corridors. People jeered. All day it was one series of fierce discussions. In the afternoon the remarks became "Strangely shocking." Well, you're nothing till you're crucified. There's one thing about bad press: it drives roots into the ground and like a tooth, you have to yank them out. Amélie's prepared to discuss her purchase offer if you withdraw from the competition. Remove her portrait from the Salon. Amélie's not a nymph you can paint nude. Don't disgrace her with this character assassination. Let the Salon take the painting down. *(**AMÉLIE** enters. **SARAH**, exiting, calls to **AMÉLIE**.)*

SARAH. *(Cont.)* Tell him how appalled you are!

AMÉLIE. You're isolating yourself. How poetic!

JOHN. You could do the same.

AMÉLIE. Can't you at least paint the strap back in? I'm so mortified—

JOHN. The portrait is realer than you. I painted with so much emotion I could barely see.

AMÉLIE. I remember...

JOHN. I thought you liked it.

AMÉLIE. I did, do, but Pedro hates it. I can't give you any money for it. What will you do?

JOHN. I won't dope myself...

AMÉLIE. The main thing I did today was choose not to take a pill.

JOHN. Good.

AMÉLIE. Don't.

JOHN. I care.

AMÉLIE. I'm starting to sniffle. Sometimes we need to hear validation—My eye makeup is dripping— Because we die inside. I had to be able to cry again, and you got me to cry and I've cried continuously for days. I cried for all the years I've lost because I did not have the courage to be anything but be beautiful. You need to remind me that being true is what I like—

JOHN. You need to spend more time with good people.

AMÉLIE. But—

JOHN. When you do so, the world will open up.

AMÉLIE. How can I when I feel so shamed?

JOHN. Humiliation is—where most of us live.

AMÉLIE. I can't go though more pain...

JOHN. You've got to stop –

AMÉLIE. I want you to talk to me more, smile more; I don't want you running from me. When I'm alone this kernel deep inside says something is missing. That's a new suffering. Being with you in the country released something. Your voice was like a little diary when I got up. It confirmed to me I was alive. I want to wake up every morning beside you—watching the breeze across the pond and the deer across the field. *(Pause).* There is a place we could meet. I don't want to lose you.

JOHN. You saw I could stop it.

AMÉLIE. I want you to take all my clothes off. Lie on top of me. *(***SARAH*** enters with the mail and* **DR. LOVE.***)*

DR. LOVE. So much negative mail.

SARAH. One mistake in Paris, you're that mistake for life.

DR. LOVE. To remove the portrait, the Salon needs this form notarized.

SARAH. Sign it. And rectify the situation..

JOHN. *(To* **AMÉLIE.***)* The art world doesn't care about you or me.

SARAH. We're at the point all subtlety is gone. Short of clubbing John over the head, there's no shortcut.

DR. LOVE. *(To* **JOHN.***)* If you keep that portrait up, I will sue you. I'm your sponsor and—

JOHN. Viper! Somebody ought to defang you. *(Scoops up stones and throws them.)* Get out. All of you. *(***DR. LOVE, SARAH,*** and* **AMÉLIE** *exit.* **OSCAR** *and* **HENRY** *enter.)*

HENRY. Why are you throwing rocks?

JOHN. The activity calms me.

OSCAR. Come to the house. Judith's arrived.

HENRY. Some people are loyal. Oscar and I have attended all your shows gleeful a foreigner was outwitting Paris. I'm American and Oscar's Irish and we've succeeded as imports in London.

OSCAR. If you have charm nothing else matters. If you don't have charm, nothing else matters. *(A sensual glimpse passes from* **OSCAR** *to* **JOHN,** *who turns awkwardly away.)*

JOHN. Leave me be. *(Exits.)*

HENRY. Shouldn't we talk to John? Try to convince him to—

OSCAR. Rule. With men who have a history of bachelorhood you can't push them. You want them to take the time to value themselves.

HENRY. John has a lot going, so we need—

OSCAR. Sooner or later he'll figure out what he needs to give up to live here permanently with us. We spoiled him. Give him a chance to feel that was the honeymoon and now he can have a life in London. *(Using a feminine voice.)* "Yes, dear. Yes, dear." Say I love you with relative frequency. "Good night, dream of us." *(Pause)* The rest is the cold ruthless warning: stay true to your talent, stay clear-eyed about it.

HENRY. But shouldn't we ask him if he wants to settle permanently in London?

OSCAR. Never ask a man a question that requires him to give up himself to make you feel better.

HENRY. What do you mean?

OSCAR. Don't ask him a question you don't know what he will answer. Right. Remember, most men are hunters.

HENRY. It's so damn old-fashioned.

OSCAR. Evolutionary. John is out there and he has to win. If you push him into a corner, he is going to fight. It's not a thought pattern, it's an intuitive thing, and what comes out his mouth may be hurtful. If he says he is tired—

HENRY. Let him be?

OSCAR. Because that's his way. He hasn't worked it out yet, or he can't verbalize it yet. *(In a feminine voice.)* Just say, "You'll feel better. Paint tomorrow. We love you, good night."

HENRY. But I need to talk to him at length. John lives in loneliness. He doesn't see we're wayfarers too and wouldn't be jealous.

OSCAR. You are a writer. You like to spell things out. You are always analyzing emotions and context. Painters are, whatever their level of intelligence, very focused on their work, and only when they have done painting can they talk to us. At least the ones who are heterosexual. Most of them aren't verbal enough. Even the "sensitive" ones. I think it's a sexual thing but I don't want to be quoted on it. We have too many friends of different persuasions.

HENRY. But I want to tell him of our counter-attack.

OSCAR. Just swallow it. Recognize that the graveyard is a place that has meaning to him and for the foreseeable future he needs to live here. We are still new in his life.

HENRY. Not that new—

OSCAR. Not as new to us. We make a commitment and we go full out. We are writers. We are trained to do that. Painters, basically they want arm candy. That's nice. They want a model, not a problem. Partnerships are hard for painters of most generations, especially bachelors. They have great intimate relations. Let it ride. Don't press. Just keep your eyes open and be watchful. Don't press.

Scene Eight

(The graveyard. Later. JUDITH *is onstage.* OSCAR, JAMES, SARGENT *enter.)*

JOHN. The doctor and Amélie are suing me.

JUDITH. I feel your pain.

JOHN. They're afraid.

JUDITH. It's as if they stabbed me.

JOHN. Should I withdraw the painting?

JUDITH. You are a creative genius and people are envious.

JOHN. I walked too far out.

JUDITH. You're aggressive and it grates on people. So what? They are evil people and you walked into their sandboxes. We artists have to carry a knife and be prepared to fight.

JOHN. I can't deal with the pomposity of the academy.

JUDITH. You have to watch for the feet that come out to trip you. When they see you climbing, they feel guilty so they knock your ladder over. You are living a courageous peril-filled life. When you are living like that, sweetie, you're up every morning and you are on it.

JOHN. I was thinking about painting in the missing strap.

JUDITH. Oh my God. No!

JOHN. All the Salon would have to do is acknowledge some part of my work. I was a thoroughly committed student. A full day at Teach's atelier, four hours of life classes. There's a real need for someone good at the Salon and I'm not going to be there—

JUDITH. A lot of us are recovering young artists.

JOHN. I miss the known, the familiar, and friends. I've embraced these people for nine years.

JUDITH. They're in collusion against you.

JOHN. I want my old life back. Most of the time it was a safe routine.

JUDITH. Somebody is going to be sacrificed. They're going to throw a body in the fire— the one who's weakest. Stay away.

JOHN. And Amélie.

JUDITH. If it was just she and you, it could be different. But there's the doctor.

JOHN. He is a weak chunk.

JUDITH. Who got ahead because of his wife's railroad empire. Get angry. Stay angry. Pray to your ancestors who had the courage to leave.

JOHN. But I have no money.

JUDITH. You know who you are—John Singer Sargent, and what you are capable of. *(Pause)* You are following the voice inside that remains unquenched despite repeated attempts to kill it. *(Pause)* You march relentlessly towards human potential, forgetting laziness permeates our condition. *(Pause)* Because of your strength - you become a target.

JOHN. What should I do?

JUDITH. Continue to make brave choices. Understand sadness will walk beside you. Move where inspiration takes you and release lassitude. *(Pause)* For you drive hominid evolution. Your force will echo through generations. Whether you are recognized is immaterial. *(Pause)* You live for others who want to be brave, but cannot, for the future of our race. *(Pause)* You must interact side by side with the devil—and not be baked in his power—rather outshine him by your actions. He will make you clearer—this is the true reason for evil in our world. *(Pause)* You will not fail...We won't let you. There is one intelligent soul who understands your purpose and if there is one, there are more.

JOHN. To know you're not defenseless, that your ship has guns.

JUDITH. You are descended from greatness—you must be great also.

Scene Nine

(Later. The graveyard—CLAUDE with a briefcase and JOHN enter.)

JOHN. Why a lawyer's office? Someone paying you off?

CLAUDE. Actually other members of the Salon felt badly about—

JOHN. Get to the point.

CLAUDE. Come back to the bohemians.

(Sound: A carriage passes, and bells ring.)

JOHN. I don't like bells. You have that sound over there and you can't stop it. *(More bells.)* I knew when the portrait went up in Studio 31, the Salon and I were getting a divorce.

CLAUDE. You projected love on the portrait, so you think you're not loved. I can't support this portrait, but I support you.

JOHN. You're not reliable. There is no indication you're capable of loyalty.

CLAUDE. Can't you find peace in accepting our differences?

JOHN. No.

CLAUDE. You shouldn't have to function in exile.

JOHN. My whole life I lived in the wrong climate. Traveling with my family to offseason hotels—trying not to look indigent. It was a Diaspora. I was unmoored. I had no relationship with place. There was a harshness and necessarily so. I felt like a marionette.

CLAUDE. Still—If you love what you do, you have a companion inside your heart. We all miss you.

JOHN. In Paris there was a lot of pleasure in seeing the same faces. The class meant nothing. It was the everyday routine. Course schools are always asymmetrical. One likes one student more than the other and it goes back and forth—keeping the balance. Still, as difficult as the studio was, I would rather have it in my life than gone.

CLAUDE. Come back before—

JOHN. I felt lucky to have you with me. You were stable and had threads to other people. You raised the talent level by entering the room. *(Pause)* And the Salon was like a modern-day palace. People don't live like that anymore. It was a gentle pathway to the kingdom of dreams.

CLAUDE. It certainly is.

JOHN. But it doesn't take long to kill something. Ambitions die young in the souls of people. People wondered why I stayed with that entry-level art school. And after a while I wondered too.

CLAUDE. Quite a few people believed in you. They still do. *(Pause)* The artists want you to stop this dreadful episode and accept a check from Amélie for five thousand dollars for the purchase and storage of the painting. All we want is to take it down.

JOHN. And if I don't comply?

CLAUDE. Let's not --

JOHN. Tell Amélie I own the portrait and will hang it as long as I please.

CLAUDE. Tell her yourself.

*(JOHN starts to leave when **AMÉLIE** walks in shrouded in black. She is tense, fighting some inner demon. She carries a flask.)*

JOHN. How are you?

AMÉLIE. Barely alive. Only the day has changed.

JOHN. That's it.

AMÉLIE. Today is Friday and no invitations. It's been Friday all day.

JOHN. Yes.

AMÉLIE. That's what happens when you get panned, the bad part, the only bad part. *(Offers him a drink from the flask.)*

JOHN. No, thanks.

AMÉLIE. There's so much backstabbing going on in Paris, you have to watch where you sit.

JOHN. And your doctor?

AMÉLIE. He runs the Salon without opposition, and when he gets some he kills it. You look tired.

JOHN. You know what's keeping me up at night. But during the day, I'm coming into my own. I've got everybody on the run, a lot of red faces. I'm going to lie low and let the other people shoot. Save my gunpowder till the end.

AMÉLIE. Oh, John. I came prepared to keep a tiny profile but I've changed my mind. I feel like I have a big black W on my chest that says, "Witch, witch." So I started hiding in the house. I cried enough tears to fill up a river and I stayed a coward and protected my feelings. I told myself, "If he cares for you, he will do something. He will send you a—" *(Offers him another drink.)*

JOHN. No, thanks.

AMÉLIE. *(Cont.)* Last night I dreamed we were married and our ship was sailing to New Orleans. Like a tortoise it was slipping into the sea going into the deepest part. The fog spangled before us like a wonderful breath in midday. New Orleans is where I got my feelings from. The city has a human frame because I've loved it so long. We were different people there. I was strong and sweet. You were brilliant and so amazing and humble. Red had come through your hair. I saw it in the light. Everyone applauded as we walked down the street. I knew the roads. I just didn't know the names. Nothing was finished. You had made yourself special by not being able to be pinned down. We lived in the French Quarter, across from a Voodoo priestess' house, you see. It had no number so I didn't know. And we talked quietly to each other late at night. Your words jeweled in my head. You said:

JOHN. Love strips us, makes us more whole.

AMÉLIE. I'll never go back in the doll box. I'll throw everything away outside.

JOHN. There's something about you. You are happiest when you're undressed.

AMÉLIE. So I've decided to empty my clothes allowance. Name your price and I'll buy the painting. This tormented image must be...temporarily removed. *(Lights fade.)*

(JOHN exits, paces before the graveyard.)

63

Scene Ten

(*Sound of cats wailing.* **AMÉLIE** *enters.* **JOHN** *is drawing.*)

JOHN. I'm down to 2 cats. That's all I have in my life. *(Laughs)* A cat lived for 18 days on top of that tomb.

AMÉLIE. I think I'm a cat. *(Purrs)* I'll let you know when you can touch me, scratch me and stroke my back.

JOHN. I look at you with a renewed sense of wonder. You're so audaciously sensual.

AMÉLIE. *(Purrs)* Move with me to New Orleans.

JOHN. Before...I didn't want another second to pass because I'd be that much closer our leaving...We lived the way you looked. It was very dreamy. I loved being in your soft world of skin. After "the annihilation" I too wore black because I was in mourning and I wanted you to die so you'd leave me alone. *(A quiet look passes between them)*

AMÉLIE. People don't realize the power of criticism. A few hundred murders is nothing for critics. They know their job is to rip the crowd into a frenzy.

JOHN. You've got your drawl back.

AMÉLIE. Insomnia. It wasn't me who didn't like the painting. It was everyone else.

JOHN. When they insulted my painting, it was like the blood of the lamb. They raided my heart. Afterwards, I had to walk around with a handkerchief to my mouth, because my nausea was so pronounced.

AMÉLIE. In New Orleans people have suffered.

JOHN. I acknowledge I'm part of that city in terms of loss.

AMÉLIE. There, you could allow yourself to...breathe.

JOHN. Maybe I could tolerate it...and survive.

AMÉLIE. Let's leave tonight. Aren't their times that are bald for you? That make you cry.

JOHN. Artists have no place for weakness. You're either strong or you're done.

AMÉLIE. In New Orleans we could recover. When we move to our own house, you'll get stronger.

JOHN. No closer! Knowledge has changed the person I am. You believe I can do anything: attack, retreat, RELOCATE?

AMÉLIE. I think you're... original. Cause I never know what you're doing.

JOHN. I can't have a future in two countries.

AMÉLIE. Return to America. Be proud to bring that gold home to Louisiana.

JOHN. Great artists have to leave America.

AMÉLIE. In New Orleans, we could shed our skin. Get under a shower and wash it off.

JOHN. Don't romanticize flight.

AMÉLIE. You'll paint better in New Orleans. Being there in lovely weather is like being in touch with God. In the midst of the hottest part of the summer, it's joyously green.

JOHN. I don't know why I keep waiting to not have this joy.

AMÉLIE. On the way to nirvana they say the girl you elope with is the one you painted.

JOHN. *(Kissing her, caving in)* But I'll have to slow the paintings down so I can sleep.

AMÉLIE. Some say you live in New Orleans you're picked by God. *(They embrace)*

Scene Eleven

(SARAH *enters with a chimpanzee under a blanket)*

SARAH. Come along Amélie... I've enough distractions what with the sickness of my chimpanzee. Somehow a rubber band got in its cage and it stopped its ability to breathe. The doctor extracted the rubber band but the chimp refuses to eat. I'm on the bottom of worry. We must get back to Paris.

AMÉLIE. I . . John and I are moving to--Louisiana.

SARAH. Oh my God!

JOHN. It's something that has to be checked out. It's not in the, "Oh my God" category.

SARAH. Well, I've been looking for a new artist to adopt, and I start to feel like a puppy when I see you and John. It's ironic. I don't know a lot about him but ...I desperately want you two to be happy...I suppose failure and its accompanying misery is the most vital source of sexual energy.

JOHN. Who says I failed? *(A cat wails)*

SARAH. Only animals that survive in darkness dwell in graveyards. Good that John isn't like the other ex-patriots who want to get in on a handshake and never leave. He's embracing the sea change. *(To* **JOHN** *and* **AMÉLIE** *)* Gentle light will carry you two to New Orleans. You'll make your genes go to the stars –

JOHN. *(To* **SARAH***)* You knew about our departure! *(To* **AMÉLIE** *)* You two discussed this.

SARAH. Don't scream.(*Anxiously*) My chimp is trembling.*(To* **JOHN***)* You must prolong the exquisite feeling running through your bodies. Amélie has always yearned to go back to New Orleans with someone special-- (**EMILY** *and* **JUDITH** *enter suddenly.)*

EMILY : You're not moving to New Orleans?!

SARAH. *(To* **EMILY***)* Who's that? I've a vague--

EMILY. I don't have a card. I'm too young to be self-conscious.

JUDITH . *(To* **SARAH***)* We're here to see John, not you.

SARAH. I'm the godmother. I've much invested to feel slammed by.

EMILY. *(To* **JOHN***)* You can't move.

JUDITH. Amélie's a Southern belle. A Southern belle has to do this—

EMILY. But not you!

JOHN. We need to find a place for us both to land.

EMILY. *(Whispers to* **JOHN***)* I thought you hated her--

JUDITH. What about your talent?

EMILY. In Paris, the tide could turn—

SARAH. Try not to be so chatty with your gratuitous remarks. What John does for work is finally his business. *(To* **JOHN***)* Your colleagues are these rapacious people. I tried to introduce some clarity into the situation. In New Orleans, you can paint the exotic. As your godmother by association, I'm seriously concerned about your stability *(To* **AMÉLIE** *and* **JOHN***)* and the 2 of your having a fruitful relationship-- The severe impact of tension on your hearts and nervous systems! You young people are either exhausted or exhausted and irritable. Not your wonderful relaxed selves. I don't think your health is going to last. Living still in your own melodrama. If you stay in Europe, you'll be losers on a level I never ever thought of. *(To* **AMÉLIE** *)* Come to the carriage. *(To* **JOHN***)* Casanova, we'll be waiting. *(***SARAH** *exits with* **AMÉLIE** *)*

JUDITH : *(To* **JOHN***)* Sarah understands Eros very well.

EMILY. (*To* **JOHN***)* When Amélie's ready to move, it'll be John who?

JOHN. Quiet. So many people have screwed me; I can tell what evil ones would do--I've fought cynicism by being sweet and smiling but Amélie's not faking it--

EMILY. It's all about fooling people. Coming round the back door. Amélie's venomous like a scorpion fish. Remember those ones we saw on the beach... with their poison loaded spears! Fish pretending to be rocks while their spines injected poison into barefoot waders.

JOHN. *(Tries to exit)* Excuse me. I've got to get my things--

JUDITH. (*Stopping him*) Moving solves some small problem though it creates a bigger one...

EMILY. New critics are reviewing the portrait.

JUDITH. Most find Amélie ugly—But <u>like</u> your style--

JOHN. I'm tired of painting. Maybe once a day I have an "Ah HA" feeling from the first line of a —I feel uninspired, bored, all written out, no new thoughts to spur me on, no audience eager for images. Wonder what my style is. Can I be so dense, so brief there's nothing there? In Paris, painters are so caught up in their work. I want to laugh at them and say "Do you really have a new idea worth expressing? Come on."

JOHN. Excuse me. (**JOHN** *exits.* **JUDITH** *and* **EMILY** *are alone)*

JUDITH. Why can't John move to Oscar's? Or Henry's –

EMILY . He could just paint there and do it for a long time.

Scene Twelve

*(*OSCAR *and* HENRY *enter)*

OSCAR. Did we hear our names?

HENRY. It's bizarre but everyone's collecting in a graveyard.

OSCAR. John has star power.

HENRY. Even now, people want to be round the fire.

EMILY. But John feels so glum.

HENRY. I was anticipating a great swirl of comedy--

OSCAR. --with all of the carriages about.

JUDITH. John is moving to New Orleans.

OSCAR. Wha-t? WHY?

HENRY. I'm not interested in why, I'm interested in WHEN.

EMILY. Right away.

JUDITH. John feels guilty.

OSCAR. He shouldn't feel guilty. He should feel horrified.

EMILY. And he's broke.

OSCAR. Good! When painters don't need money the intensity goes--

HENRY. And when the intensity goes, the quality suffers.

JUDITH. He wants to forget the feeling of loss--

EMILY. A little sooner than we want him to.

JUDITH. Let's go find him! (**EMILY** *and* **JUDITH** *exit*)

OSCAR: *(Sexually)* I was confused in a mundane way in the beginning-

HENRY. Spiritual crises usually come up in the middle of the night.

OSCAR: John won't improve things by--

HENRY. Moving to New Orleans with Amélie--

OSCAR. She's a girl with lots of walls up, and you can't—

HENRY. Break that down after a few nights of mediocre sex.

OSCAR. I'm so sick of sweating. If you want to stay starched in a graveyard forget it.

JOHN. *(Entering, suddenly)* I suppose you heard I'm leaving the country. In art, we die a little each day and then are reborn in a different disguise. *(Clearing throat)* So what's the word from Paris about my status with newer critics?

HENRY. *(Nervous)* Right now it's one level--

JOHN: *(Uneasy)* And that level is?

OSCAR: Tenuous.

HENRY. Discriminatory-

OSCAR: But fluid.

JOHN. No city blames and claims you like--

HENRY. London! We've rented you a studio next door to us.

OSCAR. Say yes to taking it easy--

HENRY. And *being aware* of--

OSCAR. *A new creativity here!*

HENRY. You're a great painter but--you don't realize--

OSCAR. Amélie is dangerous

HENRY. --and the doctor will kill you.

OSCAR. This is the polite round. Next round the knives come out.

HENRY. Come *chez nous* and wait.

OSCAR. You have many admirers whom we suspect will write soon on your behalf.

JOHN. I can't wait any longer. I'm in my dim years. I've been dead five weeks here, that's enough. I'm at the heart of tragedy in Europe—live or dead I lose.

(JOHN exits. JUDITH and EMILY enter)

EMILY. How can we keep John from leaving the country?

JUDITH. Should we pressure more critics to applaud Madame X?

EMILY. Should we go back to Paris?

OSCAR. No! Making meetings in person has not upped our success rate–

HENRY. Of getting good reviews.

OSCAR. When MEN fall in love with *(Pause)* a painting–

HENRY. They fall in love with the *(Awkward)* the--

OSCAR. *(Sensual)* Painting. And no matter how we try to make MEN –

HENRY. Fall in love with John--

OSCAR. By bragging about him in person, it doesn't help...We've done meetings and--

HENRY. The rave reviews we've gotten--

OSCAR. Have been out of *(Pause)* MEN--

HENRY. Falling in love with--

OSCAR. The painting.

HENRY. MEN. None of whom

OSCAR. We've ever had meetings with. The MEN who've extensive meetings—

HENRY. Are the type of MEN who—Take meetings and—

OSCAR. Don't end up doing anything.

OSCAR. They want to MEET because they're unsure—

HENRY. The MEN who, don't MEET are— the ones who, are getting things done.

EMILY. So you're saying that—

OSCAR. There is a certain level of— not needing a good review That is attractive— When CRITICS hear about a painting.

HENRY. We try to be very working class. But it's all about the portrait.

JUDITH. I'll go get more reviews.

EMILY. I'll help. (**JUDITH** *and* **EMILY** *exit)*

HENRY. These strong, strong women.

OSCAR. *(Referring to* **EMILY***)* That one's amphibious which makes her even stronger.

HENRY. You're going to have to boss the thing through with critics who don't care.

OSCAR. Create more *tools* to reach more people?

HENRY. Some you may find distasteful.

OSCAR. Let me go back and enlist John. I'll pretend I'm Harry Houdini or Dorian Gray?

HENRY. No. We'll reconvene!

OSCAR. If he comes to the studio and lives near us—

HENRY. Take a nap.

OSCAR. I need direct dialogue, a seduction, something I can hear from John that says--

HENRY. Don't push. I told you--painters are more interested in--

OSCAR. Facts given outside of interrogation--I –

HENRY. When you vomit up too much talk, it increases his tension.

OSCAR. I need to track his imagination.

HENRY. You need to diffuse--DIFFUSE. He doesn't need to get to the truth right away.

OSCAR. Yeah. Yeah. It's the dropping of clues that's the game.

HENRY. The whole episode drags for me too because he's so in our viewership.

OSCAR. Smart, good looking, unattainable.

HENRY. Screwed up wonderful.

HENRY. We must work harder. Get critics as invasive as he is closed off.

OSCAR. It's kind of an interesting pathology. Helping the last Virgin in London.

(**HENRY** and **OSCAR** exit.)

Scene Thirteen

(AMÉLIE enters)

AMÉLIE. *(Calling out)* John? Are you ready? Sarah's waiting--

JOHN. *(Entering, with sketchpad)* Move back. . .

AMÉLIE. To take us to the ship.

JOHN. Already? How long have you and Sarah discussed—

AMÉLIE. *(Confused, racing)* There's a privacy of--of conversation and a privacy of relation—

JOHN. You're in a frenzy.

AMÉLIE. I speed up when you're here.

JOHN. You knocked over my easel.

AMÉLIE. People are waiting. I'm letting you know we—we--We need to leave.

JOHN. Slow down.

AMÉLIE. *(Slurring, fast)* It's hard to slow down. Everything ...is speeded up. *(Dizzily) And I'm dizzy.* It only happens sometimes, it doesn't happen all the time. *(AMÉLIE pops a pill)* I take enzymes to help me digest my food. I've some kind of imbalance... Can't eat right. *(Points to stomach)* Worst parasites are from strawberries in Belgium.

JOHN. What medicine have you been using--

AMÉLIE. *(Trips)* I don't know what I'm . . . but I feel it working.

JOHN. What's in the bottle? *(Grabs bottle, reads)* Arsenic?

AMÉLIE. *(Laughs)* The standard remedy for parasites is arsenic. The epic cure...the language of the time before of legends. I know I'm slurring my words but I...need you to --leave...It's our only chance for--happiness *(Holds up a swig)* Kiss me. In olden times it was forbidden to fight in the presence of mistletoe.

JOHN. How can we talk about New Orleans ...as *our* place...with you like...I've been looking for you through many eyes in every painting but I see ruin in your face. It's reasonable to hold there's a future in America but I'm an artist. I'm always looking for causal relationships. Babies are born; old people die; death is everywhere. What is the purpose of our leaving–now?

AMÉLIE. To grow spiritually...to learn how to love.

JOHN. What happens when we do?

AMÉLIE. We transcend. Become more loving.

JOHN. ...why live in New Orleans.

AMÉLIE. We could grow in love there, we can't do that anywhere. When we're in touch with our inner bliss our love will never be lost. You must experience the real me and come from that dimension. *(Kisses him impetuously)*

JOHN. *(Laughs)* You're the last thing I'd have wanted as a man but the shrewdest thing. Fine. Here's the bargain: Bare your soul to me, I'll protect you, complete the circle, and leave.

Scene Fourteen

(*DR. LOVE enters with champagne*)

DR. LOVE. I've got the steamer tickets. Show me the talent, I'll pay the freight.

(*AMÉLIE cringes behind* **JOHN**)

JOHN. *(To* **AMÉLIE** *)* What's wrong? *(To* **DR. LOVE***)* You're like a tuning fork changing the vibrations of all around you.

DR. LOVE. I'm also in line with this cosmic vibration. I've had a change of heart. As a doctor I try to breathe facilitation. I applaud your leaving for--

AMÉLIE. *(Nervous)* Sarah told...you....?

DR. LOVE. (*To* **JOHN***)* How about a congratulatory drink--?

JOHN. You're all decked with riches. The last I knew you hated my painting.

AMÉLIE. We've no time for... champagne.

DR. LOVE. You can drink well. It takes a little more energy and a little more money. *(Sound of carriage bells)*

JOHN. *(To* **AMÉLIE** *)* I was expecting an Iago-like seduction. I like him better this visit than last.

AMÉLIE. (*Aside, to* **JOHN***)* Still ...I can feel him come at us. It's a slow creep, not a chainsaw in the face.

DR. LOVE. (*Pops the champagne)*There's an energy coming from this incredible ambrosia. Amélie why don't you swan out. *(To* **JOHN***)* So we can talk man talk.

AMÉLIE. I want to forget about gender so--

DR. LOVE. (*To* **JOHN**) She's so dismissive of me in the company of you. *(Handing him the glass.)*

JOHN. The champagne's...so gold – almost apricot. The color of the intellect.

DR. LOVE. And the color of Pluto. The god of money. (*Lifts the glass)* To your trip! (*Sound of carriage bells)*

AMÉLIE. *(To* **JOHN***)* We'll got to go to... the ship!

JOHN. (*To* **DR. LOVE***)* I'm afraid my painting will end on your wall. I need some written guarantee to insure the painting will stay hung when I leave.

DR. LOVE. I'll get a signed notice from the salon-

JOHN. Can I trust you? I don't want to hear about a fight about the painting. That it was ripped, stolen, destroyed.

DR. LOVE. I'll protect your painting. (*Picks up the glass)* A toast to renewal. I've seen artists I've (*Pause)* reconsidered and they act like my reversal is inevitable.

AMÉLIE. *(To* **DR. LOVE***)...but you said John should worship your--your*

DR. LOVE. *(To* **JOHN***)* Take that wired up girl...but watch your time --

AMÉLIE. *Stop mocking me.* You don't want my time. You want... John's glory. You've godfathered and rallied people...round you to keep...keep John in place--speaking in code like I don't know the rules. *(Sound of carriage bells)* Sarah will buy the painting for me and John. *(To* **JOHN**) Come along ... *What's... wrong? Don't you love me?*

JOHN. *I don't know.* I'm a vagabond. I don't love a thing. I walk around with a blanket. Therefore I can grab this flower this germ of the entire universe, look at it for hours, and paint it. *(Holding up the glass)* Here's to the cycle of love and loss. I've watched lovers go by wailing after the death carts. Wondering what happened to the spirit of their beloved; where it went. I'm not sure I know who you are. (*Raising glass)* Lets drink to the death of love.

AMÉLIE. Don't swallow that. *(Breathy)* It's poison. He wants you to...to faint so...he could put you on... the... the boat.

JOHN. Ah ha. Rich people have very few friends, and they usually will betray them in battle. *(***DR. LOVE** *takes out a knife. They fight.)*

DR. LOVE. I use this to open scabs, cut skin; one day I'll kill a rat.

JOHN. Go away! The both of you. It's not a barter. It's a take-over. Out! Out! *(Grabbing the knife)* I'm through with graveyards. I'm becoming my own role model. Articulate. Defiant. I want to become me when I grow up. *(Exits, laughing)*

Scene Fifteen

(JOHN bumps into **CLAUDE**, *entering)*

CLAUDE. You're leaving--. How good is God!

JOHN. But I'm not going back...

CLAUDE. I just got these telegrams. Critics are--

JOHN. Reassessing the portrait.

CLAUDE. Come watch it return to--

JOHN. Its rightful glory? That will come--

CLAUDE. But I want to see it in my lifetime--

JOHN. I can't go back *(Points to his clothes)* Like--

CLAUDE. I don't think anyone pities you. I feel people need reminding you are there. In Paris, centuries and centuries of conflict at every level of art are focusing on the painting. Talent is good, but attracting more and more champions to it is even better. *(JOHN picks up a scarf* **AMÉLIE** *has dropped.)*

JOHN. Amélie's scarf. Her moon is in cancer which is a nice place for the moon to be.

CLAUDE. You still love her--?

JOHN. I can't go back, look at the portrait, see her in that... pose.

CLAUDE. She wanted you to immortalize her.

JOHN. I gave shape to the soul of this siren--.

CLAUDE. You never knew Amélie.

JOHN. Even now I feel her!

CLAUDE. She was aligned to men who follow secret laws. But...I expect she'll retreat then return...Paris is a comeback place.

JOHN. For some. I like crossing off each day I live...without her.

CLAUDE. I'll wait for you at Oscar's. I can't take this humidity.

(**CLAUDE** *exits)*

Scene Sixteen

(The graveyard, London. **JOHN** *and* **JUDITH** *enter the stage.* **EMILY** *enters, followed by* **HUGO** *and* **WAGNER** *with fanfare.)*

EMILY. We came for the party.

JUDITH. It's not a party; it's a decadence festival.

JOHN. I can be as decadent as anyone.

OSCAR. I try to come late so you'll know no matter what happens, I'll always be there.

EMILY. They're rescinding the lawsuit. The Parisians are retreating. Crowds have been demanding to see the portrait. Some bridge oceans for 2 minutes before it. Your public wants the painting rejudged and put on permanent display.

JOHN. What?

JUDITH. You've conquered the British press.

JOHN. Holy—fantastic!

OSCAR. Those who don't have strong opinions, who are not locked up, may touch John's sweater.

HENRY. *(Enters, reading a paper.)* The London Gazette printed Oscar's review.

OSCAR. "Sargent is a master. Gautreau, a visionary beauty."

EMILY. Harper's says, "Sargent's portrait triumphs—"

JUDITH. You gave, gave, gave, and now you are going to get, get, get.

JOHN. Still more reviews?

HENRY. "Sargent's picture has a knock-down truth—"

OSCAR. That's what I wrote!

JOHN. *(Reads.)* "A wonderful rendering of life—"

OSCAR. "Beside him, his competitors stammer..."

JUDITH. I said that.

EMILY. This is just the beginning.

OSCAR. I don't want to talk about a revolution, but it's coming.

HENRY. Sargent is in training. His idea of painting is going to rebuild the world.

OSCAR. *(Reading.)* In eight hours, he was praised by thirty-nine critics. That's four-and-a- half an hour.

JUDITH. The Salon is getting you rejudged.

EMILY. After talking to the committee, I walked out with a spring in my step.

JOHN. You did what?

EMILY. Someone had to represent you to the jury. The public is causing a riot. Pounding the doors to Studio 31. They line up at dawn, sleep out front—Claiming the portrait has Italianate influence and sourcing it to the "Florence of your birth..." They say nature, living and breathing, is reflected in your portrait.

JOHN. It makes me feel good to hear the destruction going on.

JUDITH. They are calling you the greatest portrait painter of the Third Republic.

JOHN. I can't believe it.

EMILY. Commissions are pouring in from—

JUDITH. Museums all over the world.

OSCAR. The portrait's got a cult following

HENRY. Some are calling it "Madame X."

JOHN. I removed Amélie's name.

EMILY. You can lease the portrait.

JUDITH. And live off the proceeds—

EMILY. The rest of your life. What do you say?

HENRY and **OSCAR.** Melancholy Dane.

JOHN. I guess it's the best painting I've ever done.

ALL. Scandal has brought you fame. (**AMÉLIE** *enters in the portrait pose and dress of MADAME X)*

AMÉLIE. My portrait didn't ruin John's career but it ruined mine. I had more paintings done by famous artists who tried to please, putting me in white, in cream. No portrait could rival John's. I tried to buy it back for phenomenal fees using that as an excuse to see him again but he never complied. From then on he was thrust in the vortex of his dazzling career. And I the most beautiful girl in Paris because the unknown MADAME X.

END OF PLAY

Also by
Rosary Hartel O'Neill...

The Awakening of Kate Chopin

Black Jack: The Thief of Possession

Degas in New Orleans

John Singer Sargent and Madame X

A Louisiana Gentleman

Marilyn/God

Property

Solitaire

Turtle Soup

Uncle Victor

White Suits in Summer

The Wings of Madness

Wishing Aces

Please visit our website **samuelfrench.com** for complete
descriptions and licensing information.

www.ingramcontent.com/pod-product-compliance
Lightning Source LLC
Chambersburg PA
CBHW070641120726
47909CB00004B/1535